Ballerina Bess

By Dorothy Jane Mills
A.K.A. Dorothy Z. Seymour

Illustrated by
Harry Devlin

Published by
Patrician Publications
Naples, Florida

Orders to Trafford Publishing, www.Trafford.com

© 2002 by Dorothy Jane Mills. All rights reserved.
Illustrated by Harry Devlin
Published by Patrician Publications, Naples, Florida
New edition 2003.

National Library of Canada Cataloguing in Publication

Mills, Dorothy Jane
     Ballerina Bess / Dorothy Jane Mills aka Dorothy Z. Seymour ; illustrated
by Harry Devlin.

ISBN 1-55369-714-6
1. Readers (Primary). I. Devlin, Harry II. Title.

PE1119.M46 2002   428.6   C2002-903101-X

Order this book online at www.trafford.com
or email orders@trafford.com

Most Trafford titles are also available at major online book retailers.

© Copyright 2019 Dorothy Jane Mills.

All rights reserved. No part of this publication may be reproduced, stored in a retrieval system, or transmitted, in any form or by any means, electronic, mechanical, photocopying, recording, or otherwise, without the written prior permission of the author.

Print information available on the last page.

ISBN: 978-1-5536-9714-5

Because of the dynamic nature of the Internet, any web addresses or links contained in this book may have changed since publication and may no longer be valid. The views expressed in this work are solely those of the author and do not necessarily reflect the views of the publisher, and the publisher hereby disclaims any responsibility for them.

Our mission is to efficiently provide the world's finest, most comprehensive book publishing service, enabling every author to experience success. To find out how to publish your book, your way, and have it available worldwide, visit us online at www.trafford.com

Any people depicted in stock imagery provided by Getty Images are models,
and such images are being used for illustrative purposes only.
Certain stock imagery © Getty Images.

Trafford rev. 10/23/2018

 www.trafford.com

North America & international
toll-free: 1 888 232 4444 (USA & Canada)
fax: 812 355 4082

A Message from the Author

Back in 1965, when I was teaching reading to first-graders, I began writing books to help them become independent readers. These books used only a few words to tell enjoyable little stories. They gave the children practice in figuring out words on their own. I didn't realize that they would also become classics, beloved by children who cherished them, carried them around constantly, hugged them in bed, and re-read them until their families could recite them by heart and the books themselves collapsed in tatters.

These children have grown up and want to share their favorite little storybooks with their own children. The first to be republished was *Ann Likes Red*, brought out by Purple House Press in the Fall of 2001. Now the others are being reprinted, starting with *Ballerina Bess*, a simple story written with only 25 words and beloved by many little girls who learned to read with it. I hope you will like it, too.

The other titles in the series, to be reprinted later, are *The Tent, The Rabbit, Big Beds and Little Beds, The Pond, Stop Pretending, Bill and the Fish, Brad and Neil,* and my personal favorite, *The Sandwich*.

Happy reading!

Dorothy Jane Mills, A.K.A. Dorothy Z. Seymour

This is Bess.

Bess wants to dance.

"I want to
be a ballerina,"

said Bess.

"I want a ballerina dress,"

said Bess.

Dance, Bess.

Dance, Bess, dance.

This is the dress.
It is red.
It is satin.

A red satin
ballerina dress!

Bess danced.

Bess bent.

Bess sat.

Bess stood.

Bess danced in the red satin ballerina dress.

Made in the USA
Middletown, DE
29 October 2023

41553771R10015